My Magical Unicorn
COPY COLOUR BOOK

DREAMLAND PUBLICATIONS
J-128, Kirti Nagar, New Delhi -110 015, India
Tel : +91-11-2510 6050, 2543 5657
E-mail : dreamland@dreamlandpublications.com
Shop online at www.dreamlandpublications.com
Follow us on www.instagram.com/dreamland.publications

STAY
Magical

Magic
is
Everywhere

Make YOUR OWN magic

You are Magical

iT'S A
Magical
TiME

Magic
MOMENT

MAGIC

sweet dreams

MAGIC
happens

Believe
in
magic

magic
magic

Magic
is
SOMETHING
YOU MAKE

Let
THE MAGIC
Begin

YOU ARE
Magical

Make
TODAY
Magical

Sometimes
WE NEED
A LITTLE
magic

sweet
dreams

magic